AYITI

First Edition
Copyright 2011
ISBN 978-1-4507-7671-4
Photographs by Nicole Gay
Cover and interior design by Ryan W. Bradley

Stories in this collection previously appeared in the following publications: *decomP, Quick Fiction, Guernica, Necessary Fiction, Tarpaulin Sky, Weave, The Caribbean Review of Books, trnsfr,* and *Best American Erotica 2004.*

Artistically Declined Press
Oregon - New York

for my mother and father

CONTENTS

MOTHERFUCKERS

Gérard spends his days thinking about the many reasons he hates America that include but are not limited to the people, the weather, having to drive everywhere and having to go to school every day. He is fourteen. He hates lots of things.

On the first day of school, as he and his classmates introduce themselves, Gérard stands, says his name, quickly sits back down and stares at his desk, which he hates. "You have such an interesting accent," the teacher coos. "Where are you from?" He looks up. He is irritated. "Haiti," he says. The teacher smiles widely. "Say something in French." Gérard complies. "Je te deteste," he says. The teacher claps excitedly. She doesn't speak French.

Word spreads through school quickly and soon, Gérard has a nickname. His classmates call him HBO. It is several weeks until he understands what that means.

Gérard lives with his parents in a two-bedroom apartment. He shares his room with his sister and their cousin Edy. They do not have cable television, but Edy, who has been in the States for several months longer than Gérard lies and tells him that HBO is Home Box Office, a TV channel that shows Bruce Willis movies. Gérard hates that they don't have cable but loves Bruce Willis. He is proud of his nickname. When the kids at school call him HBO, he replies, Yippee Kai Yay.

Gérard's father does not shower every day because he has yet to become accustomed to indoor plumbing. Instead, he performs his ablutions each morning at the bathroom sink and reserves the luxury of a shower for weekends.

Sometimes, Gérard sits on the edge of the bathtub and watches his father because it reminds him of home. He has the routine memorized—his father splashes his armpits with water, then lathers with soap, then rinses, then draws a damp washcloth across his chest, the back of his neck, behind his ears. His father excuses Gérard, then washes between his thighs. He finishes his routine by washing his face and brushing his teeth. Then he goes to work. Back home, he was a journalist. In the States, he slices meat at a deli counter for eight hours a day and pretends not to speak English fluently.

In the second month of school, Gérard finds a bag of cheap colognes in his locker. For HBO is written on the front of the bag in large block letters. It is a strange gift, he thinks, and he hates the way the bag smells but he takes it home. Edy rolls his eyes when Gérard shows his cousin his gift, but takes one of the bottles of cologne. His girlfriend will enjoy it. "Those motherfuckers," Edy says. He is far more skilled at cursing in English. Then Edy explains what HBO means. Gérard clenches his fists. He decides that he hates each and every motherfucker he goes to school with. The next morning, he applies cologne so liberally that it makes his classmates' eyes water.

When they call him HBO, he adds a little something extra to his Yippee Kai Yay.

About My
FATHER'S Accent

He knows it's there. He knows it's thick, thicker even than my mother's. He's been on American soil for nearly thirty years, but his voice sounds like Port-au-Prince, the crowded streets, the blaring horns, the smell of grilled meat and roasting corn, the heat thick and still.

In his voice, we hear him climbing coconut trees, gripping the trunk with his bare feet and sandy legs, cutting coconuts down with a dull machete. We hear him dancing to *konpa*, the palm of one hand resting against his belly, his other hand raised high in the air as he rocks his hips from side to side. We hear him telling us about Toussaint L'Ouverture and Henri Christophe and the pride of being first free black. We hear the taste of bitterness when he watches the news from home or calls those left behind.

When we, my brothers and I, mimic him, he smiles indulgently. Before every vowel an "h", at the end of every plural, no "s."

"You make fun, but you understand me perfectly, don't you?" he says. We nod. We ask him to say *American Airlines*. We gasp for air when he gives in.

For many years, we didn't realize our parents had accents, that their voices sounded different to unkind American ears. All we heard was home.

Then the world intruded. It always does.

Voodoo CHILD

When my college roommate learns I am Haitian, she is convinced I practice voodoo, thanks to the Internet in the hands of the feeble-minded. I do nothing to dissuade her fears even though I was raised Catholic and have gained my inadequate understanding of the religion from the Lisa Bonet movie that made Bill Cosby mad at her.

In the middle of the night, I chant mysteriously, light candles. By day, I wear red and white, paint my face, dance possessed. I leave a doll on my desk. It looks just like my roommate. The doll is covered with placed strategically pins. I like fucking with her. She gives me the bigger room with the better dresser. She offers to take my tray to the dish room in the dining hall.

We take the bus to Manhattan to shop and dance and drink and hook up with dirty New York boys. I am the devil she knows.

As we emerge from Grand Central, a large, older woman runs up to me, grabs my arm, starts bowing furiously.

My mother always told me: back away slowly from crazy people; they are everywhere. When she first came to the States, she had to live in the worst part of the Bronx, the part of that borough burned beyond recognition. She hasn't yet recovered.

There, in front of Grand Central, my roommate clung to my arm her fingers digging deep, drawing blood as if I were better equipped to handle the situation.

As we backed away, I realized the woman was speaking in Creole. I didn't know her but I knew her. *Ki sa ou vle*, I asked her. She told me I was a famous *mambo*. She said it was such a pleasure to see me in America. She grabbed my wrists. She kissed my palms, held them to her cheeks. She wanted, I think, to be blessed. I was still imagining all the dirty New York boys my roommate and I would later find.

There is No "E" in
Zombi WHICH MEANS
There Can Be No You
OR We

[a Primer]

[Things Americans do not know about zombis:]

They are not dead. They are near death. There's a difference.
They are not imaginary.
They do not eat human flesh.
They cannot eat salt.
They do not walk around with their arms and legs locked
stiffly.
They can be saved.

[How you pronounce zombi:]

Zaahhhhnnnnnn-Beee. You have to feel it in the roof your
mouth, let it vibrate. Say it fast.

The "m" is silent. Sort of.

[How to make a zombi:]

You need a good reason, a very good reason.

You need a pufferfish, and a small sample of blood and hair
from your chosen candidate.

Instructions: Kill the pufferfish. Don't be squeamish. Extract
the poison. Just find a way. Allow it to dry. Grind it with the
blood and hair to create your *coup de poudre*. A good chemist
can help. Blow the powder into the candidate's face. Wait.

[a Love Story]

Micheline Bérnard always loved Lionel Desormeaux. Their parents were friends though that bonhomie had not quite carried on to the children. Micheline and Lionel went to primary and secondary school together, had known each other all their lives—when Lionel looked upon Micheline he was always overcome with the vague feeling he had seen her somewhere before while she was overcome with the precise knowledge that he was the man of her dreams. In truth, everyone loved Lionel Desormeaux. He was tall and brown with high cheekbones and full lips. His body was perfectly muscled and after a long day of swimming in the ocean, he would emerge from the salty water, glistening. Micheline would sit in a cabana, invisible. She would lick her lips and she would stare. She would think, "Look at me, Lionel," but he never did. When Lionel walked, there was an air about him. He moved slowly but with deliberate steps and sometimes, when he walked, people swore they could hear the bass of a deep drum. His mother, who loved her only boy more than any other, always told him, "Lionel, you are the son of L'Ouverture." He believed her. He believed everything his mother ever told him. Lionel always told his friends, "My father freed our people. I am his greatest son."

In Port-au-Prince, there were too many women. Micheline knew competition for Lionel's attention was fierce. She was attractive, petite. She wore her thick hair in a sensible bun. On weekends, she would let that hair down and when she walked by, men would shout, "Quelle belle paire de jambes," *what beautiful legs* and Micheline would savor the thrilling taste of their attention. Most Friday nights, Micheline and her friends would gather at Oasis, a popular nightclub on the edge of the Bel Air slum. She drank fruity drinks and smoked French cigarettes and wore skirts revealing just the right amount of leg. Lionel was always surrounded by a mob of adoring women. He let them buy him rum and Cokes and always sat at the center of the room wearing his pressed linen slacks and dark t-shirts that showed off his perfect, chiseled arms. At the end of the night, he would select one woman to take home, bed her thoroughly, and wish her well the following morning. The stone path to his front door was lined with the tears and soiled panties of the women Lionel had sexed then scorned.

On her birthday, Micheline decided she would be the woman Lionel took home. She wore a bright sundress, strapless. She dabbed perfume everywhere she wanted to feel Lionel's lips. She wore high heels so high her brother had to help her into the nightclub. When Lionel arrived to hold court, Micheline made sure she was closest. She smiled widely and angled her shoulders just so and leaned in so he could see everything he wanted to see within her ample cleavage. At the end of the night, Lionel nodded in her direction. He said, "Tonight you will know the affections of L'Ouverture's greatest son."

In Lionel's bed, Micheline fell deeper in love than she thought possible. Lionel knelt between her thighs, gently massaging her knees. He smiled luminously, casting a bright shaft of light across her body. Micheline reached for Lionel, her hands thrumming as she felt his skin. When he was inside her, she thought her heart might stop it seized so painfully. He whispered in her ear, his breath so hot it blistered her. He said, "Everything on this island is mine. You are mine." Micheline moaned. She said, "I am your victory."

He said, "Yes, tonight you are." As he fucked her, Micheline heard the bass of a deep drum.

The following morning, Lionel walked Micheline home. He kissed her chastely on the cheek. As he pulled away, Micheline grabbed his hand in hers, pressing a knuckle with her thumb. She said, "I will come to you tonight." Lionel placed one finger over her lips and shook his head.

Micheline was unable to rise from her bed for a long while. She could only remember Lionel's touch, his words, how the inside of her body had molded itself to him. Her parents sent for a doctor, then a priest, and finally a mambo which they were hesitant to do because they were a good, Catholic family but the sight of their youngest daughter laying in bed, perfectly still, not speaking, not eating, was too much to bear. The mambo sat on the edge of the bed and clucked. She held Micheline's limp wrist. She said, "Love," and Micheline nodded. The mambo shooed the girl's parents out of the room and they left, overjoyed that the child had finally moved. The mambo leaned down, got so close, Micheline could feel the old woman's dry lips against her ear. When the mambo left, Micheline bathed, dabbed herself everywhere she wanted to feel Lionel's lips. She went to Oasis and found Lionel at the center of the room holding a pale, young thing in his lap. Micheline pushed the girl out of Lionel's lap and took her place. She said, "Just one more night," and Lionel remembered her dark moans and the strength of her thighs and how she looked at him like the conquering hero he knew himself to be.

They made love that night, and Micheline was possessed. She dug her fingernails in his back until he bled. She locked her ankles in the small of Lionel's back, and sank her teeth into his strong shoulder. There were no sweet words between them. Micheline walked herself home before he woke. She went to the kitchen and filled a mortar and pestle with blood from beneath her fingernails and between her teeth. She added a few strands of Lionel's hair and a powder the mambo had given her. She ground these things together and put the *coup de poudre* as it was called into a silk sachet. She ran back to Lionel's, where he was still sleeping, opened her sachet, paused. She traced the edge of his face, kissed his forehead, then blew her precious powder into his face. Lionel coughed in his sleep, then stilled. Micheline undressed and stretched herself along his body, sliding her arm beneath his. As his body grew cooler, she kissed the back of his neck.

They slept entwined for three days. Lionel's skin grew clammy and gray. His eyes hollowed. He began to smell like soil and salt wind. When Micheline woke, she whispered, "Turn and look at me." Lionel slowly turned and stared at Micheline, his eyes wide open, unblinking. She gasped at his appearance, how his body had changed. She said, "Touch me," and Lionel reached for her with a heavy hand, pawing at her until she said, "Touch me gently." She said, "Sit up." Lionel slowly sat up, listing from side to side until Micheline steadied him. She kissed Lionel's thinned lips, his fingertips. His cold body filled her with a sadness she could hardly bear. She said, "Smile," and his lips stretched tightly into something that resembled what she knew of a smile. Micheline thought about the second silk sachet, the one hidden beneath her pillow between the pages of her bible, the sachet with a powder containing the power to make Lionel the man he once was—tall, vibrant, the greatest son of L'Ouverture, a man who filled the air with the bass of a deep drum when he walked. She made herself forget about that power; instead, she would always remember that man. She pressed her hand against the sharpness of Lionel's cheekbone. She said, "Love me."

Things I Know ABOUT
Fairy Tales

When I was very young, my mother told me she didn't believe in fairy tales. They were, she liked to say, lessons dressed in fancy clothes. She preferred to excise the princesses and villains and instead concerned herself with the moral.

Once upon a time, not long ago, I was kidnapped and held captive for thirteen days. Shortly after I was freed, my mother told me there was nothing to be learned from what had happened to me. She told me to forget the entire *incident* because there was no moral to the story.

Little Red Riding Hood didn't see the danger she was facing until it was too late. She thought she was safe. She trusted. And then, she wasn't safe at all.

My husband Michael and I, while visiting my parents in Port-au-Prince, decided to take our son to the beach for the afternoon. As we backed out of their long, narrow driveway, three black Land Cruisers surrounded us. In the end, the details of the *incident* were largely irrelevant. What was done could not be undone.

On that day, Michael and I looked at each other. We knew what was happening. Kidnapping is all anyone with any kind of money talks about in Haiti, everyone in a fragile frenzied state wondering when it will be their time. It was a relief, in a sense, to know that my time was up—to know that this day was the day I would be taken.

Two men with dark, angry faces broke the car windows with the butts of their rifles. The man on my side reached through the broken glass, unlocked my door and pulled me out of our car. He sneered at me, called me *diaspora* with the resentment that Haitians who cannot leave hold for those of us who did. His skin was slick with sweat. There was no place for traction. When I tried to grab onto the car door, he slammed the butt of his gun against my fingers. The man on Michael's side hit him in the face and he slumped forward, his forehead pressed against the horn. They put a burlap sack over my head and shoved me into the backseat of one of the waiting cars. They told me, in broken English, to do as they said and I would be back with my family soon. I sat very still. The air was stifling. All I heard was their laughter, my son crying and the fading wail of the car horn.

My father is fond of saying that a woman's greatest asset is her beauty. Snow White had her beauty, and her beauty was her curse until it became her greatest asset.

Before the *incident* my mother and I often had frank conversations about being kidnapped. She was always very concerned with the logistics because she's a woman of manners and grace. It's the kind of quotidian conversation you have in a place where nothing makes sense and there is no respect for life. She told me she wouldn't be able to survive the indignity. I told her she would have to do whatever was necessary to get through it because we needed her. As I sat between two angry men, being jostled as we sped over the broken streets of Port-au-Prince, I remembered that conversation. I realized my arrogance.

Sleeping Beauty was cursed by her birthright, by her very name. In one telling, her fate was sealed by Maleficent before she ever had a chance. Even hidden away, she could not escape the curse placed upon her.

I couldn't take it personally, being kidnapped. That is what I told myself. It was a business transaction, one that would require intense negotiation and eventually, compromise. One of the accountants who worked for my father, Gilbèrt, was kidnapped the previous year. His kidnappers originally asked for $125,000, but everyone knew it was simply a starting number, an initial conversation. Eventually, with professional assistance and proof of life, his family paid $53,850 for Gilbèrt. My negotiations would be somewhat more complex and far more costly. A good family name comes at a high price.

After the first days of my abduction, when negotiations began in earnest, I understood that the money my family would pay for my safe return was not for me. It was for the daughter, wife, mother they had last seen. I had become a different person. It seemed, somehow, unfair for them to not get what they were paying for.

After the *incident*, when Michael and I returned to the States, a throng of reporters greeted us, waiting just past the crowded, suffocating customs area in the Miami airport. Reporters lined the street where we lived. They followed us for weeks until a white woman went missing and my story no longer mattered.

The thing about Rapunzel was that she had the means to her own salvation all along. If she had only known that, she would have never been cast out by the enchantress and been forced to wait to enjoy her ever after with her prince.

My family hired an American firm that specializes in negotiating for U.S. citizens who have been abducted abroad. They were efficient. Within 24 hours, they had demanded proof of life. I was able to call my husband from a disposable cell phone. I said hello. At first, it was a relief to hear his voice, to remember his smile, the softness of his lower lip, the way he always wanted to hold my hand. But then, he started blathering about how I was going to be okay and that he was going to do everything in his power to get me back. I hung up because he was lying and he didn't know it.

Although my kidnapping was a business transaction, my captors enjoyed mixing in pleasure at my expense. I fought, but I also begged them to use condoms. I did what I had to do. Worse things could have happened. I was not broken. That's what I tell myself now, when I close my eyes and see their white teeth leering at me. It's what I tell myself when I smell their stink and their sweat or remember the weight of their thin, sinewy bodies on top of mine, taking things that weren't theirs to take. It's what I tell my husband when he thinks he wants to know what *really* happened. It is mostly true.

My parents' friend, Corinne LeBlanche, was kidnapped not long before I was taken. She and her husband and four children lived in Haiti year round. She always swore, to anyone who would listen, that if she were ever kidnapped, her husband Simon best meet her at the airport with her passport and children once she was returned because she would never spend another night in the country. Simon was a fat, happy, prominent businessman who owned a chain of restaurants and gas stations that did quite well. He laughed when Corinne made such declarations. He didn't yet understand that these things went differently for women. She and the children now live in Miami. She called me when Michael and I returned to the States. Even though we said very little, we spoke for a long time.

My kidnappers took me to a small, two-story house without air-conditioning in a cramped neighborhood on the outskirts of Cite de Soleil. They kept me in a back room furnished with a small cot and a green paint bucket filled with brackish water. Throughout the day, I could hear children playing on the street below, music from a house near by, a car now and again, the occasional gunshot. I didn't scream or try to escape. There would be no point. Anyone I might run to would just as soon take me for themselves rather than rescue me because compassion wasn't as valuable as *une diaspora*.

Two years ago, the matriarch of the Gilles family was kidnapped. She was 81. The kidnappers knew the family had more money than God. They failed to realize she was frail and diabetic. She died soon after she was abducted. Everyone who knew her was thankful that her suffering was abbreviated, until the kidnappers, having learned the lesson that the elderly are bad for business, kidnapped her grandson, who at 37 promised to be a far more lucrative investment.

At least Cinderella had her work to keep her busy—the familiarity of sweeping floors and washing windows and cooking the daily bread. If nothing else, because she had truly suffered she could appreciate her ever after.

What you cannot possibly know about kidnapping until it happens to you is the sheer boredom of being kept mostly alone, in a small, stifling room. You start to welcome the occasional interruption that comes with a meal or a bottle of water or a drunken captor climbing atop you to transact some pleasure against your will. You hate yourself for it, but you crave the stranger's unwanted touch because the fight left in you is a reminder that you haven't been broken. You haven't been broken.

Beauty learned to love the Beast. She forced herself to see past the horror of his appearance, past his behavior, past the circumstance of how they came to know one another.

On the tenth night, Ti Pierre lies next to me, staring at the ceiling. He tells me his name, after he's had his pleasure and I've had my fight. His skin is caked beneath my fingernails and my body is stiff. A bruise is forming along my jaw. I cling to the edge of the bed, trying to create as much distance as possible between our bodies until I regain the energy to fight, to remind myself that I am not broken. Ti Pierre talks to me about his life, his young son, how he wants to be a nightclub deejay because he loves American hip hop music. "We could be friends, maybe," he says, "We are close in age." I roll onto my side and bite my knuckles. He rests a tender hand on my back and I cringe, repulsed. It is the closest I will come to crying. These are the things I will never tell anyone.

At a dinner party once, with some of my colleagues and some of Michael's and lots of wine and music and excellent food and pretentious but engaging conversation, talk turned to Haiti. Everyone leaned forward in their seats, earnest in their desire to be genuine in their understanding of the world.

One of my colleagues mentioned a magazine article he read about how Haiti had surpassed Colombia as the kidnapping capital of the world. Another colleague told us about a recent feature in a national magazine. Soon everyone was offering up their own desperate piece of information, conjuring a place that does not exist.

On the fourth day of my captivity, I thought about that silly evening, and the new bits and pieces my friends were adding to their portrait. Three years later, I would overhear one of these colleagues, trying to be charming at a cocktail party, telling a precocious graduate student that he knew someone who had been kidnapped in one of *those* Third World countries. When I walked by, he wouldn't have a strong enough sense of shame to look away. Instead, he would tip his wine glass in my direction before taking a long sip and continuing to regale his audience with the few lurid details he knew.

My kidnappers and my family's negotiators finally came to an agreement on the thirteenth day. My kidnappers shared the news gleefully. I could hear them in the next room, talking about all the things they were going to do with their money. Their plans were modest, really, which made it all so much worse. They wielded cartel-like precision, and for a long while the only sound I could hear was the bills sliding against each other as they were counted into $1,000 stacks. This is what my worth sounds like, I thought. How lucky I am.

A Cuban friend once told me of a popular lullaby from her country, about a mother with thirteen children. The mother kills one child to feed twelve, so on and forth, until she is left with one child, whom she also slaughters. Finally, she returns to the middle of a cornfield where she slaughtered the other children, and slits her own throat because she cannot bear the burden of having done what needed to be done. After telling me this story, my Cuban friend said, "A West Indian woman always faces such choices."

When my kidnappers were satisfied that I had been properly bought and paid for I was cleaned up, shoved into the back of the Land Cruiser, and dropped off in the center of an open market in Pètionville. I stood there in what remained of my shirt and my filthy jeans, my feet bare, my hair a mess. My hands were in my pockets, my fingers clenched into tight fists. I stood there and waited. I tried to breathe. I was not broken. I remember these details more than any others. Around me, men and women haggled over chicken and vegetables and water and Cornflakes and radios. I was invisible, until I wasn't—until I heard my husband shout my name and run toward me with a group of men I didn't recognize. As Michael moved to embrace me, I stepped back. His expression, in that moment, I also remember. "You're safe now," he told me as if he understood the meaning of the word.

Alice had choices in Wonderland. Eat me, drink me, enjoy tea with a Mad Hatter, entertain the Queen of Hearts, down, down the rabbit hole.

I didn't speak for hours, not when I saw my parents or my child, who patted my cheeks with his chubby, wide-open hands. I took a long shower. I washed my hair and tried to scrub away the stink and sweat that comes with being trapped in a dark, hot place with strange angry men. Michael came into the bathroom to check on me, and when he saw the bruises, the weight I had lost, the bowed frame of my body, he gasped. I wrapped my arms around my body. "Get out," I hissed. "I'm not broken."

Afterward, I took my soiled clothes to the fire pit behind my parent's house and smoked cigarette after cigarette while I watched the clothes burn. For years, I had hidden my smoking from my parents, told them I'd quit, but that lie no longer seemed necessary. We ate dinner together that night, as a family, acid burning my throat with each bite. Everyone watched me intently. I smiled politely, tried to give them what they needed.

In bed that night, Michael lay on his side, watching me as I sat on the edge of the bed. "When you're ready to talk, I'm ready to listen," he said. His tone was so kind it made me nauseous. I wanted to tell him that I wasn't the woman he married, that I knew things now. Instead, I nodded and kissed his shoulder. After he fell asleep, I slipped next door into the room where Christophe slept. I picked him up, inhaled the scent of soft skin, and sat on the floor, watching as his lower lip quivered and his tiny chest rose and fell with his rapid baby breaths.

My husband found me the next morning, asleep on the floor holding our son. "You don't have to be so strong. You can cry," he said over breakfast, as if I were waiting for his permission. I didn't know how to tell him that I felt nothing at all. I held myself together until three days later, after we said goodbye to my parents under the watchful eye of their new security detail and boarded our flight to Miami. The plane took off. My chest tightened because I knew I would never really get away from that place. "Are you okay?"

Michael asked, brushing his fingers across my cheek. I shook my head, got up, and locked myself in the first class bathroom. After I threw up, I stared at the stranger in the mirror. I imagined going down, down the rabbit hole of my own happily ever after.

You Never Knew HOW THE WATERS Ran So Cruel So Deep

DATE	ITEM(S)	PRICE
18 Mars	Two (2) pairs of Phat Farm Jeans, received from your favorite uncle in Boston for your 21st birthday	1,250 gourdes, sold to your best friend Henri who is gonna look like a real gangsta, man, in his new denim
4 Avril	Collection of Michael Jackson compact discs, a gift from your father, in Brooklyn, last seen or heard from four years ago	340 gourdes sold to the old man next door, who always makes nasty comments about your girlfriend and sits in front of his house, bare-chested all day long
7 Avril	Yamaha keyboard, well-used from when you started a band and vowed to become more famous than Wyclef or Sweet Micky	$60 US, sold to your band mate, Innocent who is not a very good guitar player and hopes the keyboard will bring better fortune
23 Avril	1992 Toyota Camry, cardboard rear view window, no spare tire, rear doors don't open, axles need to be replaced	$175 US, also to your best friend who promises to drive the car as well as you have all these years
1 Mai	1/3 share in the house your father built with his two hands, where you were born, where you and your brothers played, and .35 hectares of land	$7500 US, sold to your brothers and their wives who refuse to pay you what your share is worth because they're angry you are leaving

3 Mai	Money belt to wear around the waist, the better to hide your money with	$58 US, bought from a UN soldier who does a little commerce on the side
	Concealable knife with five-inch blade, because you've heard stories about what happens on boats drifting in the middle of dark oceans	$111 US, bought from the same UN soldier who does a little commerce on the side
4 Mai	Passage for you and your wife on a somewhat seaworthy vessel from Cap-Haitien to Provinciales, Turks & Caicos, then the United States	$3250 US, bought from a smuggler who deals in all manner of cargo
6 Mai – 17 Mai	Daily levy for continued passage on the boat	$375 US, bought from a smuggler who deals in all manner of cargo
11 Mai	3 cans of sardines, 1 bar of chocolate, 2 bottles of water	4,000 gourdes, bought from a fellow passenger who brought extra provisions for this very purpose
14 Mai	Continued passage and not being thrown overboard when the boat begins taking on water and the captain needs to reduce weight	Two hours alone with your wife in the captain's quarters, sold to the captain, and two other men

18 Mai	Not being sent to a detention center upon being apprehended by a US Coast Guard cutter off the coast of North Carolina	$1500 US, bought from two enterprising Coast Guard officers who quickly learned that looking the other way can be lucrative
2 Juin	Forged papers	$750 US, bought from a guy your uncle knows
3 Juin	One month's room/board	$600 paid to your favorite uncle with whom you and your wife are living until you find a place of your own.
26 Juin	Over the Counter Sleeping Pills; small bottle of rum	$16.99 to help you and your wife sleep, to forget, bought from CVS
26 Juin	EPT Pregnancy Test	$13.95, bought from CVS

NOTE: 1 US Dollar = 40.25 Haitian Gourdes

Cheap, FAST, Filling

When Lucien arrives in the United States by way of a trip to Canada, an illegal border crossing, and hitching rides down to Miami, his cousin Christophe, who made his own way to Miami years earlier hands him a 50 dollar bill and tells Lucien to eat Hot Pockets until he gets a job because they are cheap, filling and taste good. Lucien sleeps on the floor in an apartment he shares with five other men like him, all of them pretending this is better than that which came before. There is a small kitchen with an electric stove that has two burners and a microwave that is rarely cleaned. Christophe tells Lucien that Hot Pockets are easy to prepare.

Lucien is in the United States because he loves Miami Vice. He loves the shiny suits Tubbs and Crockett wear. He loves their swagger. He loves the idea of Miami as a perfect place where problems are always solved and there are beautiful women as far as a man can see. In *secondaire,* Lucien would daydream about Miami while the French nuns frowned and slapped his desk with their rulers. He has not yet seen that Miami but he knows it is there. It has to be.

Lucien's apartment is in Pembroke Pines—a world away from Little Haiti and everything that might be familiar in an unfamiliar place. Every morning, he wakes up at five, showers, gets dressed. He walks four miles to the Home Depot on Pines Boulevard where he waits for contractors to cruise through the parking lot looking for cheap, fast labor. He stands in the immigrant bazaar with the Mexicans and Guatemalans and Nicaraguans, sometimes a few Chinese. They stand tall, try to look strong, hope that a long white finger will curl in their direction. Three or four times a week, he is lucky. He grabs his tool belt, hauls himself into the truck bed and enjoys the humid morning air as he is driven to big white houses owned by big white people locked behind gates to keep things safe from people like him.

Once a week, Lucien buys a calling card for $25. It will allow him to talk for 28 minutes. He calls home where he talks to his mother, his uncle, his wife, his four children. He tells elaborate fables about his new life—how he's found them a new home with a bedroom for each child, and air-conditioning so they can breathe cool dry air. There is a lawn with green grass and a swimming pool in the backyard by which his wife can lay in the sun. His children, two boys and two girls all under the age of ten, clamor for his attention. He strains to understand them through the static on the line. They tell him about school and their friends and the UN soldier who is renting a room in the house, how he's teaching them Brazilian curse words. When there are only a few minutes left, his wife chases the children into the bedroom they all share. They are alone. There is no time for anything tender. She whispers that she needs Lucien to send more money, there's no food, there's no water. She wants to know when he will send for them. He lies. He tells her he's doing all he can. He says *soon*.

On the weekends, Christophe picks Lucien up in the truck his boss lets him take home and they go to house parties in Little Haiti. They listen to *konpa* and drink rum and as all Haitians are wont to do. They philosophize about

54

how to solve their country's problems. "Haiti," his father would always tell Lucien while he was growing up, "is a country with seven million dictators." Sometimes, when it is very late at night, Lucien will find comfort in the arms of a woman who is not his wife. He will go home with her and in the darkness, as he cups her breasts with his hands, and listens to her breathing against him, as he presses his lips against her neck, and her shoulder, then licks the salt from her skin, he will imagine she tastes like home.

Around the corner from Lucien's apartment is a 7-11. Sometimes, when he can't sleep, Lucien likes to go to there because it is cool and bright and white and clean and he can buy Hot Pockets. The man who works there late at night is also Haitian. He understands why Lucien likes to walk slowly up and down each aisle, carefully studying each row filled with perfectly packaged products. When the clerk first arrived in Miami, he did the same thing. Lucien thinks about the sweet things he would buy for his children if they were with him and how much it would please him to watch them eat a Twix or a Kit Kat. Each night, before he leaves 7-11, Lucien buys two Hot Pockets that he microwaves, and a Super Big Gulp. He walks home and sits on the curb in front of his building so he can be alone. He drinks slowly, so slowly there's no ice left in the cup when he's done. He eats one of the Hot Pockets and the other one, he holds. He enjoys its warmth, thinks he's holding the whole of the world in his hands.

In the Manner OF WATER or Light

My mother was conceived in what would ever after be known as the Massacre River. The sharp smell of blood has followed her since. When she first moved to the United States, she read the dictionary from front to back. Her vocabulary quickly became extensive. Her favorite word is *suffuse*, to spread over or through in the manner of water or light. When she tries to explain how she is haunted by the smell of blood, she says that her senses are *suffused* with it.

My grandmother knew my grandfather for less than a day.

Everything I know about my family's history, I know in fragments. We are the keepers of secrets. We are secrets ourselves. We try to protect each other from the geography of so much sorrow. I don't know that we succeed.

As a young woman, my grandmother worked on a sugarcane plantation in Dajabón, the first town across the border Haiti shares with the Dominican Republic. She lived in a shanty with five other women, all strangers, and slept on a straw mat beneath which she kept her rosary, a locket holding a picture of her parents, and a picture of Clark Gable. She spoke little Spanish so she kept to herself. Her days were long and beneath the bright sun, her skin burned ebony and her hair bleached white. When she walked back to her quarters at the end of each day, she heard the way people stared and whispered. They steered clear. They were terrified by the absence of light around and within her. They thought she was a demon. They called her *la demonia negra*.

After saying her prayers, after dreaming of Port-au-Prince and lazy afternoons at the beach and the movie house where she watched *Mutiny on the Bounty* and *It Happened One Night* and *The Call of the Wild,* after dreaming of the warmth of Clark Gable's embrace, my grandmother would tear her old dresses into long strips so she could better bind the cuts and scratches she earned from a long day in the cane fields. She would sleep a dreamless sleep, gathering the *courage* she would need to wake up the next morning. In a different time, she had been loved by two parents, had lived a good life but then they died and she was left with nothing and like many Haitians, she crossed over into the Dominican Republic in the hope that there, her luck would change.

My grandfather worked at the same plantation. He was a hard worker. He was a tall, strong man. My grandmother, late at night when she cannot sleep, will sit with a glass of rum and coke, and talk about how her hands remember the thick ropes of muscle in his shoulders and thighs. His name was Jacques Bertrand. He wanted to be in the movies. He had a bright white smile that would have made him a star.

My grandmother is also haunted by smells. She cannot stand the smell of anything sweet. If she smells sweetness in the air, she purses her lip and sucks on her teeth, shaking her head. Today, when we drive to our family's beach property in Montrouis, she closes her eyes. She can neither stand the sight of the cane fields nor the withered men and women hacking away at stubborn stalks of cane with dull machetes. When she sees the cane fields, a sharp pain radiates across her shoulders and down her back. Her body cannot forget the labors it has known.

Now, the Massacre River is shallow enough to cross by foot but in October 1937, the waters of what was the Dajabón River ran strong and deep. The unrest had been going on for days—Dominican soldiers determined to rid their country of the Haitian scourge went from plantation to plantation in a murderous rage. My grandmother did the only thing she could, burning through a long day in the cane field, marking the time by the rise and fall of her machete blade. She prayed the trouble would pass her by.

It was General Rafael Trujillo who ordered all the Haitians out of his country, who had his soldiers interrogate anyone whose skin was too dark, who looked like they belonged on the other side of the border. It was the general who took a page from the Book of Judges to exact his genocide and bring German industry to his island.

Soldiers came to the plantation where my grandmother worked. They had guns. They were cruel, spoke in loud, angry voices, took liberties. One of the women with whom my grandmother shared her shanty betrayed my grandmother's hiding place. We never speak of what happened after that. The ugly details are trapped between the fragments of our family history. We are secrets ourselves.

My grandmother ended up in the river. She found a shallow place. She tried to hold her breath while she hid from the marauding soldiers on both of the muddy shores straddling the river. There was a moment when she laid on her back, and submerged herself until her entire body was covered by water, until her pores were suffused with it. She didn't come up for air until the ringing in her ears became unbearable. The moon was high and the night was cold. She smelled blood in the water. She wore only a thin dress, plastered to her skin. Her feet were bare. When a bloated corpse slowly floated past her, then an arm, a leg, something she couldn't recognize, she covered her mouth with her hand. She screamed into her own skin instead of the emptiness around her.

Jacques Bertrand who worked hard and wanted to be in the movies found his way to the river that ran strong and deep. He moved himself through the water until he found my grandmother. He tapped her on the shoulder and instead of turning away, she turned into him, opened that part of her herself not yet numb with terror. She found comfort in the fear mirrored in his eyes. His chest was bare and she pressed her damp cheek against his breastbone. She slowed her breathing to match his. She listened to the beat of his heart; it echoed beneath the bones of his ribcage. "An angel," she told me. "I thought he was an angel who had come to deliver me from that dark and terrible place."

My grandparents bound their bodies together as their skin gathered in tiny folds, as their bodies shook violently. Jacques Bertrand, who worked hard, who wanted to be in the movies, wrapped his arms around my grandmother. In a stuttered whisper, he told her the story of his life. "I want to be remembered," he said. She cupped his face in her hands, traced his strong chin with her thumbs, and brushed her lips across his. She followed the bridges of scar tissue across his back with her fingertips. She said, "You will be remembered." She told him the story of her own life. She asked him to remember her too.

My grandmother still hears the dying screams from that night. She remembers the dull, wet sound of machetes hacking through flesh and bone. The only thing that muted those horrors was a man she knew but did not know who wore bridges of scar across his back. I do not know the intimate details, but my mother was conceived.

In the morning, surrounded by the smell and silence of death, my grandparents crawled out of the river that had, overnight, become a watery coffin holding 25,000 bodies. The Massacre River had earned its name. The two of them, soaking wet, their bodies stiff and on the verge of fever, crawled into Ouanaminthe. They were home. They were far from home. My grandmother laced her fingers with my grandfather's and they sought refuge in an abandoned church. They fell to their knees and prayed and then their prayers became something else, something like solace.

When night fell again, the Dominican soldiers crossed into Ouanaminthe, into a place they did not belong. My grandfather was killed. He saved my grandmother's life by confronting three soldiers, creating a window through which my grandmother could escape. Jacques Bertrand died wanting to be remembered, so my grandmother stayed in that place of such sorrow, took a job cooking and cleaning for the headmaster of a primary school. At night, she slept in an empty classroom. She gave birth to my mother and later married the headmaster who raised my mother as his own. At night, my grandmother took my mother to the river and told her the story of how she came to be. My grandmother knelt on the riverbank, her bones sinking in the mud as she brought handfuls of water to her mouth. She drank the memories in that water.

When my mother turned twelve, she, my grandmother, and the headmaster moved to Port-au-Prince. The school had closed and the headmaster took a new appointment in the capital. At first, my grandmother refuse to leave her memories, but the headmaster put his foot down. She was his wife. She would follow. My mother recalls how her mother wailed, her voice pitched sharp and thin, cutting everything around her. In the front yard of their modest home, a large coconut tree fell, it's wide trunk split neatly in half. The fallen fruit rotted instantly. My grandmother went to the Massacre River, her long white hair gathered around her face. She took river mud into her hands, eating it, enduring the thick, bitter taste. When my mother and the headmaster found her, my grandmother was lying in a shallow place, shivering beneath a high moon, her face caked with dry mud.

In the capital, my grandmother was a different woman, quieted. The headmaster consulted Catholic missionaries, *houngans* and *mambos* in case she had been possessed by a *lwa* or spirit, and needed healing. Finally, he resigned himself to living with her ghosts. He loved her as best a man whose wife loves another man can. He focused on my mother's education and waited. Sometimes, the headmaster asked my mother if she was happy. She said, "My mother does love you."

It wasn't until the day my mother left Port-au-Prince that my grandmother became herself again. I've been told that the headmaster and my grandmother stood on the tarmac white with heat, the air billowing around them in visible waves. My mother kissed her mother twice on each cheek. She kissed the headmaster. She turned and headed for the staircase to board the plane, a heavy wind blowing her skirt wildly. My grandmother didn't run after her only child but she did say, "*Ti Couer*." Little heart. My mother stopped. She didn't turn around.

***

My mother is a small, nervous woman. Her life began, she says, the day she got off the Pan Am flight from Port-au-Prince in New York City. She sat in the back of a yellow taxicab driven by a man who spoke a language she did not understand. She stared out the dirty window and up at the tall steel buildings. She was twenty-one. My mother found an apartment in the Bronx. She took a job as a seamstress for Perry Ellis making clothes she loved but could not afford. She learned to speak English by reading the dictionary and watching American television. Once a month, she wrote her mother and the only father she knew a long letter telling them about America, begging them to join her. My grandmother always wrote back, but refused to leave Haiti. She would not leave the ghost of a man who could not be forgotten.

My mother went to doctor after doctor trying to find someone who would free her from the sharp smell of blood that has always suffused her senses. Each doctor assured my mother it was all in her head. She took the subway to Chinatown and tried acupuncture. The acupuncturist carefully inserted needles into the webs of her thumbs, and along her body's meridians. As he placed each needle, he shook his head. He said, "There are some things no medicine can fix."

When I asked my mother how she met my father she said, "I wasn't going to marry a Haitian man." She rarely answers the question she is asked. My father is an ear, nose, and throat specialist. He is the last doctor my mother consulted. When she told him she could only smell blood, he believed her. He tried to help her and when he couldn't, he asked her to join him for dinner. Eventually he asked for her hand in marriage. She didn't say yes. She told my father she would never return to Haiti, that he would have to accept that her life began a year earlier. She was a seamstress whose senses were suffused with the smell of blood, who didn't know her father and couldn't understand her mother. They were married in a Manhattan synagogue, nine months after they met.

My parents remained childless for many years but never discussed the matter. If my mother was asked when she would start a family, she would say, "I am very much in love with my husband." When she learned she was pregnant with me, at the age of forty, it was a hot July afternoon in New York, 1978. She ran out onto to the street, threw her hands in the air, stared into the incandescent sun. She cried as the light spread over her. A joyful sound vibrated from her throat, through her mouth and into the city around her. She went to my father's office and told him the news. He cried too. When I was born, I was crying lustily. We are a family unafraid of our tears.

My mother has never been able to accept she will never know her real father. She worries her mother has woven the story of her conception into an elaborate fable to hide a darker truth. My mother has an imagination. She knows too much about what angry, wild soldiers will do to frightened, fleeing young women. My mother looks in the mirror and cannot recognize herself. She only sees the face of a man she can never know. When I was a little girl and we sat together at the dinner table, my mother often stared into the distance, grinding her teeth. My father would take her hand and say, "Jacqueline, please stop worrying." She never did. She was the keeper of her mother's secrets. She was a secret herself.

Every summer, once I turned five, my parents took me to JFK and sent me to my grandmother's for three months. I was dispatched to do the work of dutiful daughter in my mother's absence. My grandmother and the man I know as my grandfather, the headmaster who took in a scared young woman whose skin had burned ebony, whose hair had bleached white, who bore a child with no father, they were kind to me. I brought them pictures of my parents and money my mother carefully stuffed in my shoes. I brought cooking oil and pantyhose, a VCR and videotapes, gossip magazines, Cornflakes. I knew never to bring anything sweet.

My grandmother kept her promise to Jacques Bertrand. Each time she saw me, she offered new fragments of their story or, if my mother's fears were correct, her story. I looked like him, had his eyes and his chin. Like my parents, my grandmother and the headmaster doted on me. When I returned to the States at the end of each August, I would try to ask my mother questions, to better piece things together but she would only shut herself in her room, rub perfume across her upper lip, lie on her back, her eyes covered with a cool washcloth.

When I was thirteen, the headmaster drove my grandmother and I to their beach property in Montrouis for the afternoon. Just before leaving New York for the summer, I had celebrated my Bat Mitzvah. The three of us sang along to *konpa,* and the adults listened to me chattering from the back seat. It was a good day. I longed for my mother to know there was so much joy to be found in the country of her birth. As we pulled into a gas station, beggars suddenly swarmed our car, a throbbing mass of dark, shiny faces and limbs needing more than we could possibly give. There was a man with one leg and one old, wooden crutch. His face was disfigured by a bulging tumor beneath his left eye. He planted his hands against the glass of the window, leering at me, the skin over the tumor rippling with his anger. It was the first time I understood the land of my mother's birth as a place run through with pain.

Each time I returned to New York and the comforts of home, I brought pictures and long letters and special spices —these affections, mother by proxy. My mother always took me for lunch, alone, at the Russian Tea Room the day following my return. She had me recount my trip in exhaustive detail, inhaling from a perfume-scented handkerchief every few minutes, carefully probing so as to get the clearest sense of how her mother was doing. Once in a while, I forgot myself and asked my mother why she didn't just go to Haiti to find out for herself. In those moments, she gave me a stern look. She said, "It is not easy to be a good daughter."

When I turned 16 I went to summer camp in Western Massachusetts because I was young and silly. I wanted to do *normal* things. Haiti was too much work. I was tired of the heat and the smells and the inescapable poverty, how my sweaty limbs caught in mosquito netting, how I had to go to the well for water when the cistern wasn't working. I was sick of the loud hum of generators and tiny lizards clinging to window screens and the way everyone stared at me and called me *la mulatte.* Summer camp was a largely disappointing experience. I was a city girl and the Berkshires were far too rural for me. I wasn't any kind of Jewish the other girls at the camp could understand. I spent the summer sitting on the lakeshore reading, lamenting that I could have been at a real beach in the Caribbean with people who loved me and looked like me. It would be ten years before I returned to Haiti.

The next summer, my father took me to Tel Aviv. He showed me the apartment where he grew up in Ramat Aviv. He showed me his parents' graves, told me how much they would have loved me. I saw all kinds of people who did indeed look like me, who didn't laugh at my stuttered Hebrew. We spent a week on a kibbutz, my father in his linen shirt and shorts, tanned, laughing, home. I felt a real sadness for my mother who couldn't take such joy in the land of her birth. We went to the beach. We went to Jaffa and looked toward the sea and Andromeda's rock. We cried at the Wailing Wall. I understood Haiti was not the only place in the world run through with pain.

***

The year after I graduated from law school, the headmaster died. I called my grandmother to ask how she was doing. She said, "I have been a good wife." She was ready to return to Jacques Bertrand. I told my mother we had to go see her mother. She was lying on her bed, rubbing perfume across her upper lip. She had not taken news of the headmaster's death well. He was the only father she ever knew. She turned to me and said, "This is my home, where I am needed." I said,

"You are needed elsewhere," and she waved a hand limply, conceding the point.

My father prescribed my mother some Valium, and the three of us flew to Port-au-Prince. By the time we landed, my mother was sufficiently sedated. As we disembarked and walked into the terminal, she dreamily asked "Are we there?" My grandmother and her driver were waiting for us. I inhaled sharply as I saw her for the first time in a decade. She was impossibly small, a frail figure, her dark flesh much looser now, her features hollowed, her white hair swept atop her head in a loose bun. She and my mother stood inches apart and stared at each other. My grandmother took her daughter's face in her hands, nodded. That night, in our hotel, I heard my mother whisper to my father that she could hardly breathe but for the smell of blood.

After a few days in the capital helping my grandmother settle her affairs and visiting the headmaster's grave, she was ready to return to Jacques Bertrand. Despite our demand she stay in the capital or return to the States with us, my grandmother was resolute. We drove across the country to Ouanaminthe on the only passable road. It took hours and by the time we arrived, we were all tired, sweaty, sore and irritable. Ouanaminthe was not the city it had once been. It was a sad, hopeless place, crumbling buildings everywhere, paint peeling from billboards, the streets crowded with people, each person wanting and needing more than the next. Most of the roads had gone to mud from recent flooding. The air was stifling and pressed down on us uncomfortably. As we stood in the courtyard in front of the small concrete house my grandmother had purchased, men hanging from a passing Tap Tap leered at us. My father stood in front of me, glaring. My mother rubbed her forehead and asked my father for another Valium.

My mother and her mother kept to themselves for the first few days, huddled together, trying to make up for nearly thirty years of separation. There was no room for my father and I in what they needed from one another. On the second night, I went to a local bar where everyone stared as I took a seat at the bar. I drank watery rums and Coke until my face and my boredom felt numb. I danced to Usher with a man named Innocent. When I snuck back into my grandmother's house, I found her sitting in the dark. She nodded to me but said nothing. On the third night, the moon was high and bright, casting its pale light over and through everything. I lay beneath mosquito netting in a tank top and boxers, one arm over my head, one arm across my stomach, my body feeling open and loose. I listened to the sounds of everyone else sleeping. I tried to understand the what and why of where we were.

Just as I was on the verge of drifting asleep, I heard a scratching at the door and sat up, pulling the sheets around me. My grandmother appeared in the doorway. She curled her bent fingers, beckoned. Slowly, I stretched myself out of bed, pulled on a pair of jeans and flip-flops. I found my grandmother by the front door. My mother was standing next to her, fidgeting, shifting from one foot to the other, clutching at her perfume-scented handkerchief. "What's wrong?" I asked. My grandmother smiled in the darkness. "Come with us," she said.

We walked nearly a mile to the banks of the Massacre River, my grandmother pressing her hand against the small of my mother's back. In the distance, we could see soldiers keeping watch at the checkpoint, their cigarettes punctuating the darkness. I heard hundreds of frightened people who looked like me splashing through the water, searching for safety and then, silence. My grandmother climbed down the damp, steep riverbank, my mother warning her mother to be careful. She waved for us to join her. I slipped out of my sandals, took my mother's hand, helped her into the river. We stood in a shallow place. I curled my toes in the silt of the riverbed and shivered. I had pictured the river as a wide, yawning and bloody beast, but where we stood, the river flowed weakly. The waters did not run deep. It was just a border between two geographies of grief.

My grandmother pointed down. The hem of her dressing gown floated around her. "Here," she said softly.

My mother's shoulders shook but she made no sound. She gripped my arm. "I cannot breathe," she said. Then she dropped to her knees, curled into her self. She said, "I must know the truth."

I knelt behind her. I held her, tried to understand her. I said, "You can breathe." My grandmother said, "You know the only truth that matters." Again I heard hundreds of frightened people splashing through the water, keening, reaching for something that could never be reached. The ground beneath us trembled from the heavy footsteps of roving soldiers. I smelled their sweat and their confused, aimless anger.

We knelt there for a long while. My grandmother stood, whispering the story of how she came to know and remember Jacques Bertrand until her words dried on her lips. I stroked my mother's hair gently, waited for her breathing to slow, her back rising into my chest with a melancholy cadence. We mourned until morning. The sun rose high. Bright beams of light spread over and through us. The sun burned so hot it dried the river itself, turned the water into light. We were left kneeling in a bed of sand and bones. I started crying. I could not stop. I cried to wash us all clean.

Lacrimosa

Marise thought she knew things about tears. When she was a little girl in Port-au-Prince, her father would listen to Mozart's *Requiem* while their neighbors danced to *konpa* and American rock and roll. Their small two-room home would fill with the melancholy of earnest choral voices and string instruments. Whenever the *Lacrimosa* sequence began, her father would close his eyes and hold a hand high in the air. Everyone would still. The music was so beautiful Marise understood she was feeling everything that could ever be felt. Then the government was overthrown again and again and again and mouths grew hungry and an even thicker maze of wires began stretching from house to house, each family stealing power from here and there. Walking down alleys, you could no longer see the sky and then it was time for the generators with their loud angry hum making everything thick with the smell of diesel. Her father put the turntable away. There was nothing left to feel.

When the UN soldier first came to her door with his brown skin and baby blue bulletproof vest, he said his name was Carlos Rocha from Veli Velha, Brazil. He held his helmet in the crook of his arm, his long rifle slung over his shoulder. Fat beads of sweat rolled down his face. He had money, a slow, lazy grin and curly black hair. He smiled at her only child. Carlos Rocha gently squeezed the boy's cheek between the calluses of his soldier hands. He asked if she cooked, what she charged for her spare room. His grin widened, revealing dimples. She smiled back, nervous, named her price. Everything in Port au Prince had a price.

The soldier moved in. Every night, he returned to Marise's well kept home, complained about the heat, the heavy air, the trash everywhere, the dark shiny people throwing rocks and bottles and angry words. He ate her food. He shared her bed, touched her body with his soldier hands; he filled her and frightened her and she felt something she didn't understand. She learned about lachrymatory agents, how chemical compounds were designed for the express purpose of stimulating the corneal nerves to draw tears and inflict pain. He told her how his unit was once locked in a bunker filled with tear gas. The soldiers tried not to breath or cry, the jowls of their cheeks quivering uncontrollably until their chests threatened to explode and finally they sobbed not because of the burning in their eyes, nose, throat but because of the frailty of feeling everything at once. Marise sang songs to comfort the soldier after his long days patrolling dark, dangerous places. She learned his words. He learned hers. She worried.

It did not take long for Marise to forget that Carlos Rocha was a man on a mission. He was far from his home. He would not stay. The warmth of her body, the way she welcomed him inside her, the taste of her skin were all things he would walk away from. He kept a well-oiled gun beneath her bed, carried it every day, and once in a while he shot he fired he hurt he killed. She forgot all this until one day, her boy sat in front of their small concrete house, tears streaming down his face as he stacked spent tear gas canisters as high as his little arms could reach. When the boy felt his mother's shadow over him, he looked up with his bright shining eyes, holding a canister in each chubby fist. He said, "Look Mama, I made!" She remembered what was and what would not be. She pulled her child into her arms. She felt nothing but the bitterness of her son's tears on her tongue.

The Harder
THEY Come

We were told lots of things about The Americans—they want our skin bronze and our teeth white and gleaming and our shirts cut low. The Americans want us to be impressed by the size of their cruise ship and other such things. The Americans want us to speak English, but not too well. The Americans want us to smile and flatter.

Every week, we stand, perfectly groomed in a perfect line. We watch as the cruise ship slowly pulls into port. Before long, the pier fills with The Americans—some pale, some tan, mostly large and red-faced. The women wear ill-fitting bikinis and wraps and sundresses. The men wear Hawaiian shirts and board shorts and khaki shorts and tank tops. Their faces are covered with large, black sunglasses. They talk loudly. They walk slowly. As they near us, they look up at the large sign that reads, "Welcome to Labadee." They see us and say, "The local color here is just so pretty."

We serve them drinks and local foods and sell them "handmade crafts from local artisans" that arrived on another boat from China.

The Americans rent jet skis and shout to each other as they bounce over waves. Their skin bronzes and burns. The Americans are happy.

They drink and drink and drink and get louder and happier. They ask us to take their pictures and they point their cameras at us so when they return home, they can have friends over for wine to show off all the dangerous places they have been.

The Americans apply suntan lotion and bathe in the sun, stretching their bodies on striped chaise lounges and as they bake, they fill the air with the sickly sweet smell of coconut oil. They listen to music and read glossy magazines and try to decide what they want for dinner back on the boat and complain about the thick, humid air.

They say they quite like this Haiti, so clean and calm, so pleasant, not at all like on CNN. The Americans ask questions but rarely listen to the answers. Beyond the pier and the heat of the white sand beach with the striped chaise lounges and the thatched huts with brightly colored roofs there is a thick line of lush palm trees and behind the lush palm trees is a very tall fence lined with barbed wire separating this Haiti from that Haiti. The Americans never ask to see that Haiti. The Americans know that Haiti is there.

The Americans, the men, they like us and want us. They think we too are for sale as part of the Hispaniola experience. They offer us their American dollars and expect us to be impressed by the likeness of Andrew Jackson. We prefer the countenance of Benjamin Franklin. The Americans grab our asses and whisper in our ears, leaving their hot, boozy breath on our skin. The less original among them say things like, "Voulez vous couchez avec moi?" in heavy, awkward French, over enunciating each word. Some of us are indeed for sale or want to know what it would be like with a man with such pale skin or we are bored or we just don't care. We tell The Americans to follow us. We walk down the hot sandy beach slowly, shaking our hips and they ogle us and they say vulgar things we pretend not to hear. We walk until we can no longer see the pier, can no longer hear the laughter or the sharp hum of jet skis or the haggling for local crafts. We sneak behind a rocky embankment or a small thicket of palm trees or a deserted section of shaded beach.

The men, The Americans, they don't fill our heads with romantic ideas. There are no tender moments. The Americans bite our bare shoulders and squeeze our brown breasts in their meaty hands. They groan as they tell us to get on our knees, take them in our mouths. They ask us if we like it. We pretend not to speak English. We whisper silly things in French. We try not to laugh which sounds like a moan and that, The Americans adore. They fuck us from behind with our hands and cheeks pressed against the burning rocks. They fuck us behind the market or against the fence beyond the thick line of lush palm trees. They never take long. They never say thank you. The Americans, however, always come.

All THINGS
BEING Relative

The copper country of Michigan's Upper Peninsula is a forgotten place. The land is vast and densely forested, filled with ghosts and skeletons wandering through the industrial ruin. In the summer, the U.P. is breathtaking and irresistible; in the winter, blanketed by snow upon snow, ice and sand, the U.P. is unforgiving, inhospitable, inescapable.

Copper once reigned. There were mines, rich with ore and men ready, willing, able to pull that bounty from the earth. The mine owners prospered. They built grand homes atop hills, had buildings named after them. The men who worked for these mine owners did not prosper as much but they owned homes of their own and they fed their families and on Sundays they went to church to thank the God who provided all good gifts.

Progress is not kind and human nature cannot resist the lure of possibility. Where once it was man who pulled the copper from the enriched soil of the Upper Peninsula, then it was machine, and then there was no need for any of it and then there was nothing left.

There is a beauty to be found in an abandoned mine. There is also a profound sadness. Stone walls decaying into awkward angles. Machines rusted in motion. Grasses grown wild, encroaching on all things.

Old houses, haunted by miners with nothing to mine, don't fade away. They fall. They slump to their knees. They bow their heads.

We get the news here in upper Michigan—the frenzied accounts of recessions and depressions and unemployment. Things have changed, we're told. It's a new world and a new economy. People are hungry, tired, sick, poor. There is no respite—no way to satisfy our hunger or rejuvenate our spirits, heal our wounds or change our fortunes. We laugh, bitterly. This is not news.

My parents were born in Haiti, the first free black nation in the world.

It is an island of contradictions.

The sand is always warm. The water is so clear blue bright that it is sometimes painful to behold. The art and music are rich, textured, revelatory, ecstatic. The sugar cane is raw and sweet.

And yet. What most people know is this— Haiti is the poorest country in the Western Hemisphere. Her people eat mud cakes. There is no infrastructure—no sewer system, no reliable roads, erratic electricity. Women are not safe. Disease cannot be cured. Violence cannot be quelled. The land is eroding. The sky is falling.

Freedom, it seems, has a price. We are defined by what we are not and what we do not have.

We get American news in Haiti too, via CNN, beamed down from satellites. We hear about these recessions and depressions, the unemployment, how things have changed. In the background, we listen to the grinding hum of the generator, perhaps in the distance, gunshots as UN peacekeepers and roving gangs skirmish. We laugh. We marvel at such good news. The bitter taste burns.

Gracias, NICARAGUA
Y LO Sentimos

Nicaraguenses, nosotros Haitianos lo sentimos pero no
    queremos más el titulo del país más pobre en el
    hemisferio occidental. Le damos las gracias. El
    deshonor ahora es el suyo.

You should know this: every news story ever written or
    aired in perpetuity, whether on Euro News,
    Univision, ESPN or ABC, CNN, CBS, FOX or
    NBC, will begin and end referring to your beloved
    land as the poorest country in the Western
    Hemisphere. You are what you have not.

You will hear these words until you are sick to your
    stomach, until you no longer recognize *su tierra,*
    until you start to believe the news stories are true,
    that nothing else matters, that *si no puedes comprar*
    cosas que no necesitas, tu no existes, tu no cuentas, tu
    no mereces respeto.

It won't matter if the story is about Nicaraguan art or
    the food, the music or your people. It could be a
    story about wages or natural disasters, unrest in the
    countryside, the latest telenovela or *escándalo*
    político.

Por ejemplo, a blonde American reporter could be
    interviewing a famous Nicaraguan children's author.
    Her very first question undoubtedly will be, "What's

it like coming from the poorest nation in the Western Hemisphere?"

Just know, the poor author will be left standing with her brightly illustrated book, full of ideas, vim and vigor, eager to discuss *historias para los niños* and instead she will have to call upon the political science class she slept through in college to make do in her new role as political correspondent.

At least in hearing this, you know what to expect. You might also take comfort *en el conocimiento* that it likely won't take long for *Ayiti* to regain her place. *El deshonor siempre ha sido nuestro.*

The Dirt We
DO NOT Eat

Once or twice a month, Elsa in Cap-Haïtien receives a letter from her cousin Sara in Miami. The letter is thick with news and US dollars and promises of a better life, a better place, a better time, better things.

> I wish you could see South Beach. The men are more beautiful than the women. They all wear makeup and fine clothes. The beach is not like home. It is crowded. It is dirty. After work my friends and I, we run along the water barefoot. We drink straight from bottles of wine. We eat McDonalds and other good food. They put so much salt on the French fries for hours you can suck the grains from your fingers, feel them on your lips.

Elsa saves these letters in a tin box she keeps beneath the narrow bed she shares with her boyfriend who she pretends is her husband even though he has a woman on the side.

> My dearest cousin, South Beach sounds like a dream. I have never tasted wine but worry not. We still have our rum. You should know Christian is up to his old tricks, he won't work, he won't stay. I think of you often. I wait for you to steal me away.

Elsa misses Sara. She does. She hates Sara. She does. She hates the letters, the news, the promises, the lies. She hates hearing about air conditioning and water always running cold, safe to drink from the faucet and TV shows about strippers and millionaires and more.

Is it true Haitians are eating mud pies? Has it been so long since I've been home that the land itself sustains us? Last night I ate Dairy Queen. The ice cream reminded me of the poem we read when we were in *secondaire* about plums in the icebox, so cold and so sweet. I will never be able to enjoy another treat if it is true that all we have left is the ground at our feet, wet with water, a little salt, squeezed between our hands, baked in the hot sun, dry in our mouths.

Those left behind have heard these stories on Euro News and on Radio Metropole because one eager journalist saw what he wanted to see saw and old woman at the side of the road, squatting over her pies her bare knees peeking out from the folds of her skirt.

Ma chère cousine, I read your letter while walking on white sand burning my bare feet. I looked out at the water so clear blue it hurt my eyes. Last night, *maman* made us *griot* and *diri ak Pwa* and Christian who can smell a good meal from between a woman's thighs finally came home. The three of us ate together and we laughed. There wasn't much food but what there was, was enough. I'll tell you this. We do not enjoy as much food as perhaps once we did. When Christian goes to get rice from MINUSTAH, he must take his gun, three friends. Some mornings we wake, our stomachs empty, our stomachs angry, but never do we look to the ground beneath our feet with longing in our mouths. We chew on our pride. The dirt we do not eat.

What You Need to Know ABOUT A HAITIAN Woman

When his wife was a young girl, she was playing with a young chick in the yard, chasing after it, laughing, having fun. When the mother hen realized *her* child was being teased, she ran across the dusty yard and began pecking at his not yet wife's legs. His mother-in-law, upon seeing *her* child being hen-pecked, ran outside, raised the mother hen in the air and snapped its neck. Later, she had the chicken prepared for dinner. She said it was the best meal she ever ate. When the mother hens chicks grew up, she killed them too. The point, the Haitian father will then say to a potential suitor, is this: you don't need to worry about him. You need to worry about the mother.

A Cool DRY Place

Yves and I are walking because even if his Citröen was working, petrol is almost seven dollars a liter. He is wearing shorts, faded and thin, and I can see the muscles of his thighs trembling with exhaustion. He worries about my safety, so every evening at six, he picks me up at work and walks me home, all in all a journey of twenty kilometers amidst the heat, the dust, and the air redolent with exhaust fumes and the sweet stench of sugarcane. We try and avoid the crazy drivers who try to run us off the road for sport. We walk slowly, my pulse quickening as he takes my hand. Yves' hands are what I love best about him; they are calloused and wrinkled, the hands of a much older man. At times, when he is touching me, I know there is wisdom in those hands.

We have the same conversation almost every day—what a disaster the country has become, but we cannot even muster the strength to say the word disaster because the word does not describe our lives. There is sadness in Yves face that also defies description. It is an expression of ultimate sorrow, the reality of witnessing the country, the home you love, disappearing not into the ocean but into itself.

We stop at the market in downtown Port-Au-Prince. Posters for Aristide and the Fanmi Lavalas are all over the place even though the elections, an exercise in futility, have come and gone. A vendor with one leg and swollen arms offers me a box of Tampax for twelve dollars, thrusting the crumpled blue and white box towards me. I ignore him as a red-faced American tourist begins shouting at us. He wants directions to the Hotel Montana, he is lost, his map of the city is wrinkled and torn and splotched with cola. "We are Haitian, not deaf," I say. The American smiles, relaxes into the comfort of his own language.

Yves rolls his eyes and pretends to be fascinated with an art vendor's wares. He has no tolerance for *fat Americans.* They make him hungry. Hunger reminds him of the many things he tries to ignore. Yves learned English in school. I learned from television—*I Love Lucy, The Brady Bunch,* and my favorite show, *The Jeffersons* with the little black man who walks like a chicken. When I was a child, I would sit and watch these shows and mimic the actors' words until I spoke them perfectly. Now, as I tell the red-faced man the wrong directions, because he has vexed me, I mouth my words slowly, with what I hope is a flawless American accent. The man shakes my hand too hard, and thrusts five gourdes into my sweaty hand. Yves sucks his teeth as the man walks away and tells me to throw the money away, but I stuff the faded bills inside my bra. We continue to walk around, pretending we can afford to buy something sweet or something nice.

When we get home, the heat threatens to suffocate us. It always does. The air-conditioning window unit is not working because. It has been defeated by the on and off of daily power outages. The air is thick and refuses to move. I look at the rivulets of sweat streaming down Yves' dark face. I want to run away to some place cool and dry. My mother has prepared dinner, boiled plantains and *legumes,* a beef and green bean stew. She is weary, sweating, bent, nearly broken. She doesn't speak to us as we enter, nor do we speak to her.

There is nothing any of us can say that hasn't already been said. She stares and stares at the black and white photo of my father, a man I have little recollection of. He was murdered by the *Makoute,* the secret military police, when I was only five years old. Late at night, I dream of my father being dragged from our home, of his body beaten as he was thrown into the back of a large green military truck. He was the lucky one. Sometimes, my mother stares at my father so hard, her eyes glaze over and she starts rocking back and forth. I look at Yves. I know should anything happen to him, it will be me holding his picture, remembering what was and will never be. I understand our capacity to love.

We eat quickly and afterwards, Yves washes the dishes outside. My stomach still feels empty. I rest my hand over the slight swell of my belly. I want to complain I am still hungry, but I do not. I cannot add to their misery. I catch Yves staring at me through the dirty window as he dries his hands. He always looks at me in such a way that I know his capacity to love equals mine. His eyes are wide, lips parted slightly as if the words *I love you* are forever resting on the tip of his tongue. He smiles, but looks away quickly as if there is an unspoken rule forbidding such impossible moments of joy. Sighing, I stand and kiss my mother on the forehead, gently rubbing her shoulders. She pats my hand and I retire to the bedroom Yves and I share. I wait. I think about his teeth on my neck and the weight of his body pressing me into our bed. Sex is one of the few pleasures we have left. It is dark when Yves finally comes to bed. As he crawls under the sheets, I can smell rum on his breath. I lie perfectly still until he nibbles my earlobe.

Yves chuckles softly. "I know you are awake, Gabi."

I smile in the darkness and turn towards him. "I always wait for you."

He gently rolls me onto my stomach and kneels behind me, removing my panties as he kisses the small of my back. His hands crawl along my spine, and again I can feel their wisdom as he takes an excruciating amount of time to explore my body. I arch towards him as I feel his lips against the backs of my thighs and one of his knees parting my legs. I try and look back at him but he nudges my head forward and enters me in one swift motion. I inhale sharply, shuddering, a moan trapped in my throat. Yves begins moving against me, moving deeper and deeper inside me and before I give myself over, I realize that the sheets are torn between my fingers and I am crying.

Later, Yves is wrapped around me, his sweaty chest clinging to my sweaty back. He holds my belly in his hands and I can feel the heat of his breath against the back of my neck.

"We should leave," he murmurs. "So that one day, I can hold you like this and feel our child living inside of you."

I sigh. We have promised each other that we will not bring a child into this world and it is but one more sorrow heaped onto a mountain of sorrows we share. "How many times will we have this conversation? We'll never have enough money for the plane tickets."

"We'll never have enough money to live here either."

"Perhaps we should just throw ourselves in the ocean." Yves stiffens and I squeeze his hand. "I wasn't being serious."

"Some friends of mine are taking a boat to Miami week after next."

This is another conversation we have too often. Many of our friends have tried to leave on boats. Some have made it, most have not, and too many have turned back when they realized the many miles between Haiti and Miami are not so few as the space on the map implies. "They are taking a boat to the middle of the ocean where they will surely die."

"This boat will make it," Yves says confidently. "A priest is traveling."

I close my eyes. I try to breathe, yearning for just one breath of fresh air. "Because God has done so much to help us here on land?"

"Don't talk like that." He is silent for a moment. "I told them we would be going too."

I turn around and try to make out his features beneath the moon's shadows.

Yves grips my shoulders. Only when I wince does he let go. "This is the only thing that does make sense. *Agwé* will see that we make it to Miami and then we can go to South Beach and Little Haiti and watch Cable T.V."

My upper lip curls in disgust. "You will put your faith in the same god that traps us on this godforsaken island?"

"If we go we might know, once in our lives, what it is like to breathe."

My heart stops and the room suddenly feels like a big echo. I can hear Yves' heart beating where mine is not. I can imagine what Yves' face might look like beneath the Miami sun. I will follow him wherever he goes.

When I wake, I blink, covering my eyes as cruel shafts of sunlight cover our bodies. The sun never has mercy here. My mother is standing at the foot of the bed, clutching the black and white photo of my father.

"Mama?"

"The walls are thin," she whispers.

I stare at my hands. They have aged overnight. "Is something wrong?"

"You must go with Yves, Gabrielle," she says, handing me the picture of my father.

I stare at the picture trying to recognize the curve of my eyebrow or the slant of my nose in his features. When I look up, my mother is gone. For the next two weeks I work and Yves spends his days doing odd jobs and scouring the city for the supplies he anticipates us needing. I go through the motions, straightening my desk, taking correspondence for my boss, gossiping with my coworkers. I am dreaming of Miami and places where Yves and I are never hungry or tired or scared or any of the other things we have become. I tell no one of our plans to leave, but I want someone to stop us, remind me of all the unknowns between here and there.

At night, we exhaust ourselves making frantic love. We no longer bother to stifle our voices. I do things I would have never considered before; things I have always wanted to do.

There is a freedom in escape. Three nights before we are to leave, Yves and I are in bed, making love. We are neither loud nor quiet. Gently, Yves places one of his hands against the back of my head, urging me towards his cock. I resist at first, but he is insistent in his desire, his hand pressed harder, fingers tangling into my hair and taking firm hold. It becomes difficult to breathe but it also excites me, makes me wet as he carefully guides me, his hands gripping harder and harder, his breathing faster. Suddenly, he stops, roughly rolling me onto my chest, digging his fingers into my hips, pulling my ass into the air. I press my forehead against my arms, gritting my teeth. I allow Yves to enter me, whispering terrible words into the night as he rocks me. I feel so much pleasure, so much pain. The only thing I know is I want more —more of the dull ache and the sharp tingling, more of feeling like I will shatter into pieces if he pushes any further —more. Yves says my name, his voice so tremulous it makes my heart ache. It is nice to know he craves me in the same way, that my body clinging to his is a balm.

Afterwards, we lie side by side, our limbs heavy and Yves talks to me about South Beach with the confidence of a man who has spent his entire life in such a place; a place where rich people and beautiful people and famous people dance salsa at night and eat in fancy restaurants overlooking the water. He tells me of expensive cars that never break down and jobs for everyone; good jobs where he can use his engineering degree and I can do whatever I want. He tells me about Little Haiti, a neighborhood just like our country, only better because the air-conditioning always works and we can watch cable T.V. The cable T.V. always comes up in our conversations. We are fascinated by its excess. He tells me all of this and I can feel his body next to mine, tense, almost twitching with excitement. Yves smiles more in two weeks than the three years we have been married and the twenty-four years we have known each other and I smile with him because I need to believe this idyllic place exists. I listen even though I have doubts and I listen because I don't know what to say.

The boat will embark under the cover of night. On the evening of flight, I leave work as I always do, turning off all the lights and computers, smiling at the security guard, telling everyone I will see them tomorrow. It is always when I am leaving work that I realize what an odd country Haiti is, with the Internet, computers, fax machines and photocopiers in offices and the people who use them living in shacks with the barest of amenities. We are a people living in two different times. Yves is waiting for me as he always is, but today, he is wearing a nice pair of slacks and a button down shirt, the black shoes he wears to church. This is his best outfit, only slightly faded and frayed. The tie his father gave him is hanging from his left pocket. We don't talk on the way home. We only hold hands and he grips my fingers so tightly my elbow starts tingling. I say nothing, however, because I know that right now, Yves needs something to hold onto.

I want to steal away into the sugarcane fields we pass, ignoring the old men, dark, dirty and sweaty as they wield their machetes. I want to find a hidden spot and beg Yves to take me, right there. I want to feel the soil beneath my back and the stalks of cane cutting my skin. I want to leave my blood on the land and my cries in the air before we continue our walk home, Yves' seed staining my thighs, my clothes and demeanor hiding an intimate knowledge. But such a thing is entirely inappropriate, or at least it was before all this madness began. My face burns as I realize what I am thinking and I start walking faster. I have changed so much in so short a time.

My mother has changed as well. I would not say she is happy but the grief that normally clouds her features is missing, as if she slid out of her shadow and hid it someplace secret and dark. We have talked more in two weeks than in the past two years. We will write, and someday Yves and I will save enough money to bring my mother to Miami, but nothing will ever make up for the wide expanse between now and then.

By the time we reach our home, Yves and I are drenched in sweat. It is hot, yes, but this is a different kind of sweat. It reeks of fear and unspeakable tension. We stare at each other as we cross the threshold, each mindful of the fact that everything we are doing, we are doing for the last time. My mother is moving about the kitchen, muttering to herself. Our suitcases rest next to the kitchen table, and it all seems rather innocent, as if we are simply going to the country for a few days, and not across an entire ocean. I cannot rightly wrap my mind around the concept of crossing an ocean. All

I know is this small island and the few feet of water I wade in when I am at the beach. Haiti is not a perfect home, but it is a home nonetheless.

Last night, Yves told me he never wants to return, that he will never look back, and lying in bed, my legs wrapped around his, my lips against the sharp of his collarbone, I burst into tears.

"*Chère,* what's wrong?" he asked, gently wiping my tears away with the soft pads of his thumbs.

"I don't like it when you talk like that."

Yves stiffened. "I love my country and I love my people, but I cannot bear the thought of returning to this place where I cannot work or feel like a man or even breathe. I mean you no insult when I say this, but you cannot possibly understand."

I wanted to protest, but as I lay there, my head pounding, I realized I probably couldn't understand what it would be like for a man in this country where men have so many expectations placed upon them that they can never hope to meet. There are expectations of women here, but it is in some strange way, easier for us. It is in our nature, for better or worse, to do what is expected of us. And yet, there are times when it is not easier, times like that moment when I wanted to tell Yves we should stay and fight to make things better, stay with our loved ones, just stay.

I have saved a little money for my mother. It started with the five gourdes from the red-faced American, and then most of my paycheck and anything else I could come up with. This money will not make up for the loss of a daughter and a son-in-law but it is all I have. After we leave, she is going to stay with her sister in Petit Goave. I am glad for this. I could not bear the thought of her alone in this stifling little house, day after day.

I walk around the house slowly, memorizing each detail, running my hands along the walls, tracing each crack in the floor with my toes. Yves is business-like and distant as he re-makes our bed, fetches a few groceries for my mother, hides our passports in the lining of his suitcase. My mother watches us but we are all silent. I don't think any of us can bear to hear the sound of each other's voices. I don't think we know why. Finally, a few minutes past midnight, it is time. My mother clasps Yves' hands between hers, smaller, more brittle. She urges him to take care of me, of himself. His voice cracks as he assures her he will, that the three of us won't be apart long. She embraces me tightly, so tightly that again my arms go numb. I hold her, kissing the top of her head, promising to write as soon as we arrive in Miami, promising to write every single day, promising to send for her as soon as possible. I make so many promises I cannot promise to keep.

And then, we are gone. We do not look back. We do not cry. Yves carries our suitcases and quickly we make our way to a deserted beach where there are perhaps thirty others, looking as scared as us. There is a boat—large, and far sturdier than I had imagined. I have been plagued by nightmares of a boat made from weak and rotting wood, leaking and sinking into the sea, the only thing left behind, the hollow echo of screams. Yves greets a few of his friends, but stays by my side. "We're moving on up," I quip, and Yves laughs, loudly. I see the priest Yves promised would bless this journey. He is only a few years older than us. He appears painfully young. He has only a small knapsack and a Bible so worn it looks like the pages might fall apart at the lightest touch. His voice is quiet and calm as he ushers us onto the boat. Below deck there are several small cabins, and Yves seems to know which one is ours. I realize Yves has spent a great deal of money to arrange this passage. He stands near the small bed, his arms shyly crossed over his chest and I see an expression on his face I don't think I have ever seen before. He is proud, eyes watery, chin jutting forward. I will never regret this decision, no matter what happens to us. I have waited my entire life to see my husband like this. I see him for the first time.

Later, I am above deck, leaning over the railing, heaving what little food is in my stomach into the ocean. Even on the water, the air is hot and stifling. We are still close to Haiti. I had hoped the moment we set upon the ocean I would be granted one sweet breath of cool air. Yves is cradling me against him between my bouts of nausea, promising this sickness will pass, promising this is but a small price to pay. I am tired of promises, but they are all we have to offer. I tell him to leave me alone, and he is hurt, but I can't comfort him when I need to comfort myself. I brush my lips across his knuckles and tell him I'll meet him in our cabin soon. He leaves, reluctantly, and when I am alone, I close my eyes, inhaling the salt of the sea deep into my lungs, hoping that smelling this thick salty air is one more thing I am doing for the last time.

I think of my mother and father and I think that being here on this boat may well be the closest I will ever come to knowing my father, knowing what he wanted for his family. All I want is peace. I wipe my lips with the back of my hand, ignoring the strong taste of bile lingering in the back of my throat, I return below deck where I find Yves, sitting on the end of the bed, rubbing his forehead.

I place the palm of my hand against the back of his neck. It is warm and slick with sweat. "What's wrong?"

He looks up but not at me. "I'm worried about you."

I push him further onto the bed and straddle his lap. He closes his eyes and I caress his eyelids with my fingers, enjoying the curl of his eyelashes and the way it tickles my skin. He is such a beautiful man, but I do not tell him this. He would take it the wrong way. It is a strange thing in some men, this fear of their own beauty. I lift his chin with one finger and trace his lips with my tongue. They are cracked but soft. His hands tremble but he grips my shoulders firmly. I am amazed at how little is spoken between us yet how much is said. We quickly slip out of our clothes and his thighs flex between mine. The sensation of his muscle against my flesh is a powerful one that makes my entire body tremble.

I slip my tongue between his lips and the taste of him is so familiar and necessary that I am suddenly weak. I fall into Yves, kissing him so hard I know my lips will be bruised in the morning. I want them to be. Yves pulls away first, drawing his lips roughly across my chin down to my neck, the hollow of my throat, practically gnawing at my skin with his teeth. I moan hoarsely, tossing my head backwards. My neck throbs and I know that here too, there will be bruises. He sinks his teeth deeper into me and I can no longer see the fine line between pain and pleasure. But just as soon as I consider asking him to stop, he does, instead lathering the fresh wounds with the softness of his tongue, murmuring sweet and tender words. Such gentleness in the wake of such roughness leaves me shivering.

The weight of my breasts rests in Yves hands and he lowers his lips to my nipples, suckling them. He looks up at me and it is unclear whether this is a moment of passion or a moment of comfort for him, for me. And then I cannot look at him so I rest my chin against the top of his head, my arms wrapped around him, my hips slowly rocking back and forth. I want him inside me, but I wait. This moment, whatever it is, demands patience.

Yves takes hold of my knees spreading my legs wide and pushing them upwards until they are practically touching my face. I rest my ankles against his shoulders and shudder as he buries inside me. I feel his pulsing length, his sweat falling onto my body, into my eyes, mingling with mine, the tension in his body as I claw at the wide stretch of black skin across his back. Tomorrow, he too will have bruises.

"Let go," I urge him.

Then, he is fucking me faster, harder. We are greedy. I cannot recognize him. I am thankful. I scream. The sound of it is a horrible thing. I can feel wetness trailing down the inside of my arm—Yves' tears. I am tender inside but I don't want Yves to ever stop. With each stroke he takes me further away from the sorrows of home and closer to a cool dry place.

ACKNOWLEDGMENTS

I am especially grateful to the editors of the fine magazines where these pieces originally appeared. I'm also grateful for the patience of my friends, family and loved ones who indulge my writing habit even when it is inconvenient.